This book belongs to:

_____

_____

To Lucy and Nina ~ M. A.

For Mom Lynne, Peter Dad and andibles too numerous to mention xx ~ L. S.

tiger tales
5 River Road, Suite 128,
Wilton, CT 06897
Published in the United States 2015
Originally published in Great Britain
2013 by Little Tiger Press Ltd.

Text copyright © 2013 Little Tiger Press Ltd.
Illustrations copyright © 2013 Loretta Schauer

ISBN-13: 978-1-58925-457-2
ISBN-10: 1-58925-457-0
Printed in China
LTP/1400/4437/1221
All rights reserved
3 4 5 6 7 8 9 10

For more insight and activities,
visit us at www.tigertalesbooks.com

Little Red Riding Hood

adapted by Mara Alperin

Illustrated by Loretta Schauer

tiger tales

Once there was a little girl who loved to wear red. She had red shirts and red skirts, red shoes, and a fabulous bright red coat. Her name was Little Red Riding Hood.

Early one morning, Little Red's mother packed up a basket.

"I have a very special job for you," she told Little Red. "Grandma is feeling sick — will you take her this fresh fruit?"

"Of course!" cried Little Red, and she put on her favorite coat and kissed her mother good-bye.

It was a bright, sunny day, and Little Red skipped through the woods.

"Good morning!" she called to the rabbits and the deer. "I'm bringing Grandma a special surprise!"

But someone was peeking
from behind a tree . . .

. . . a big, hungry wolf!

"Good day," growled the wolf. "What are you doing in the woods all alone?"

"I'm taking this special basket of fruit to Grandma!" Little Red replied.

Yuck, thought the wolf. He didn't like fruit. *He* liked to eat tasty little girls!

So the wolf thought up a plan — a horrible, clever plan! "Why not pick Grandma some pretty flowers?" he said.

"Good idea!" said Little Red. But as she started gathering daisies, the wolf raced down the path toward Grandma's house.

The wolf knocked on Grandma's door with
a **thud! thud! thud!**

"Is that you, Little Red, my dear?" called Grandma.

"Yes!" squeaked the wolf. "Let me in — it's
breakfast time!"

"Oh, good," said Grandma, opening the door. "What are we having for breakfast?"

"YOU!" cried the wolf . . . .

"Ahhhhh!" yelled Grandma. "*You're* not Little Red!"
And she slammed the door, right on his big, furry nose.

"Ow ow OOOOOWWWWWW!"

howled the wolf.

In a flash, Grandma
ran out of the back door
and into the woods to
find help.

"That wasn't nice!"
the wolf growled,
rubbing his nose.

But now he could put his
terrible plan into action . . . .

So when Little Red knocked tap! tap! tap! on Grandma's door, it was a deep, scratchy voice that answered,

"Come in, my dear."

Little Red walked into Grandma's
bedroom and stopped in surprise.
"Why Grandma!" she said slowly.
"What BIG EARS you have!"

"The better to hear you with, my dear," croaked the wolf.

"And Grandma," Little Red said
carefully, "what BIG, HAIRY
ARMS you have!"

"The better to hug you with,
my dear," growled the wolf.

"But Grandma," Little Red whispered, "what big TEETH you have!"

And he pounced at Little Red . . . .

Just at that moment, the door burst open.
In rushed Grandma, with the woodcutter.
"Stop right there!" yelled Grandma.

"Put her down now!"
bellowed the woodcutter,
"or we'll chop you up and turn
you into a birdhouse!"

With a terrified howl,
the wolf jumped out of the
window and ran far, far away,
never to return.

Little Red hugged Grandma tight.
"I'm SO glad you chased that wolf
away!" she said. And she gave
Grandma the basket of fruit.

"What a day of excitement!"
laughed Grandma. "Now let's
all have breakfast!"

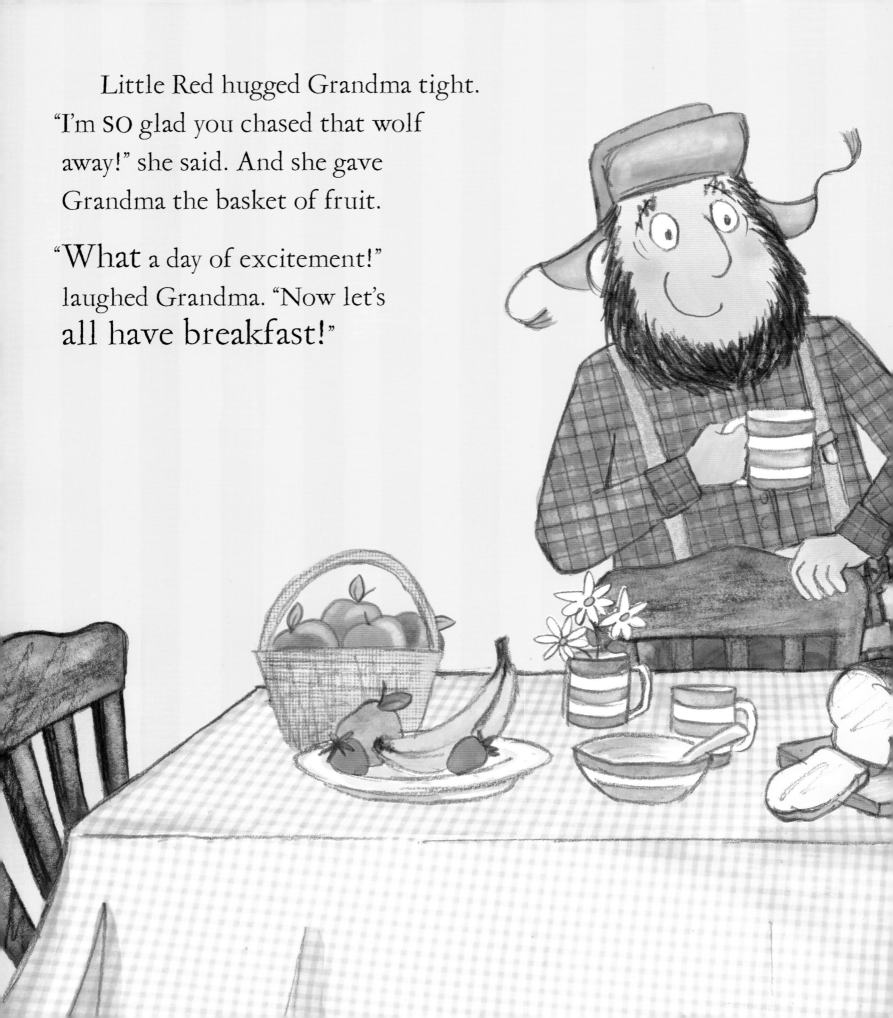